MVFOL

$BL°, 1.7$

$AR PTS: 0.5$

Dear Parent:
Your child's love of reading starts here!

Every child learns to read in a different way and at his or her own speed. Some go back and forth between reading levels and read favorite books again and again. Others read through each level in order. You can help your young reader improve and become more confident by encouraging his or her own interests and abilities. From books your child reads with you to the first books he or she reads alone, there are I Can Read Books for every stage of reading:

SHARED READING
Basic language, word repetition, and whimsical illustrations, ideal for sharing with your emergent reader

BEGINNING READING
Short sentences, familiar words, and simple concepts for children eager to read on their own

READING WITH HELP
Engaging stories, longer sentences, and language play for developing readers

READING ALONE
Complex plots, challenging vocabulary, and high-interest topics for the independent reader

ADVANCED READING
Short paragraphs, chapters, and exciting themes for the perfect bridge to chapter books

I Can Read Books have introduced children to the joy of reading since 1957. Featuring award-winning authors and illustrators and a fabulous cast of beloved characters, I Can Read Books set the standard for beginning readers.

A lifetime of discovery begins with the magical words **"I Can Read!"**

Visit www.icanread.com for information
on enriching your child's reading experience.

I Can Read Book® is a trademark of HarperCollins Publishers.

Dixie Copyright © 2011 by HarperCollins Publishers. All rights reserved. Manufactured in China. No part of this book may be used or repro-
duced in any manner whatsoever without written permission except in the case of brief quotations embodied in critical articles and reviews.
For information address HarperCollins Children's Books, a division of HarperCollins Publishers, 10 East 53rd Street, New York, NY 10022.
www.icanread.com

Library of Congress Cataloging-in-Publication Data is available.
ISBN 978-0-06-171914-1 (trade bdg.) —ISBN 978-0-06-171913-4 (pbk.)

11   12   13   14   15   SCP   10   9   8   7   6   5   4   3   2   ❖   First Edition

I Can Read!

BEGINNING
1
READING

Dixie

story by Grace Gilman
pictures by Sarah McConnell

HARPER
An Imprint of HarperCollinsPublishers

Dixie is Emma's puppy.

Every day,

Dixie waits for Emma

to come home from school.

Dixie and Emma eat snacks.

They play games.

Everywhere Emma goes,

Dixie goes, too.

One day,

Emma came home and said,

"Dixie, I am too excited

to do anything!

My class is putting on a play.

It's *The Wizard of Oz.*

And I want to be Dorothy."

WOOF!

WOOF!

9

Dixie did not understand.
But if Emma was excited,
so was Dixie.

Dixie yipped. She yapped.

She grabbed the papers

from Emma's hand.

"I need those papers," said Emma.

"They have the lines for my part!

Now be quiet, Dixie."

All day long, Emma read her lines.

Dixie tried to be good.

She sat by Emma,

quiet as can be.

She did not yip or yap

or grab.

It was hard!

"There's no place like home,"

Emma read out loud.

Then she put down the papers.

"Woof!" Dixie barked.

Maybe it was time to play!

But Emma frowned at Dixie.

"I want to be Dorothy

so badly," she said.

"What if I don't get the part?"

The next day, Dixie waited for Emma.

"Look!" Emma ran to Dixie.

She held up ruby slippers.

"I got the part!

I'm Dorothy!" said Emma.

"And you get to be my dog, Toto."

Dixie wagged her tail.

"All you have to do

is follow me everywhere,"

Emma told her.

Emma was happy!

Dixie ran.

She jumped.

Dixie could not sit still

for one more minute!

Dixie leaped in the air.

CRASH! Dixie tipped over games.

She knocked down books.

"Dixie! Stop!" Emma shouted.

"I still have to study.

The play is in three days."

19

Each day that week,

Emma studied in her room.

Each day, Dixie tried to play.

But Emma always said,

"No, Dixie!"

What could Dixie do?

She pulled out clothes.

She chewed and chomped.

"Dixie!" Emma shouted.

"This is a mess and I need quiet.

The play is tomorrow!"

"What if I forget my lines?"
Emma whispered.

"What if I mess up?"
She turned her back to Dixie
and picked up the papers to study.

Not again!

It was too much.

Dixie had to do something!

She grabbed a ruby slipper

and ran out of the room.

"Dixie!" Emma shouted.

"Bring that back!"

But Dixie didn't.

She hid the shoe.

Then Dixie hid, too.

Emma looked and looked.

She couldn't find

the slipper anywhere.

At last, she got ready for bed.

Emma was too upset to go to sleep.

"The play will be awful!"

she sobbed.

"I don't have my shoe.

I don't have my dog.

And I know I will forget my lines!"

Dixie crept closer.

Emma was upset!

Dixie had to do something.

"Woof!"

Dixie took the shoe to Emma.

"Dixie!" said Emma.

She held Dixie close.

"I really do know my lines,"
Emma told Dixie.
"Everything will be perfect."
Together, they fell asleep.

The next night was the play.

Emma was Dorothy,

and Dixie was Toto.

Everywhere Emma went,

Dixie went, too!

When it was over

everyone clapped for a long time.

Dixie barked and barked.

But Emma didn't tell her to stop.

Everything was perfect.

Back at home,

Emma and Dixie had a snack.

Then they played and played.

"There really is no place like home!"
Emma said.

Dixie licked Emma's face.

She thought so, too!